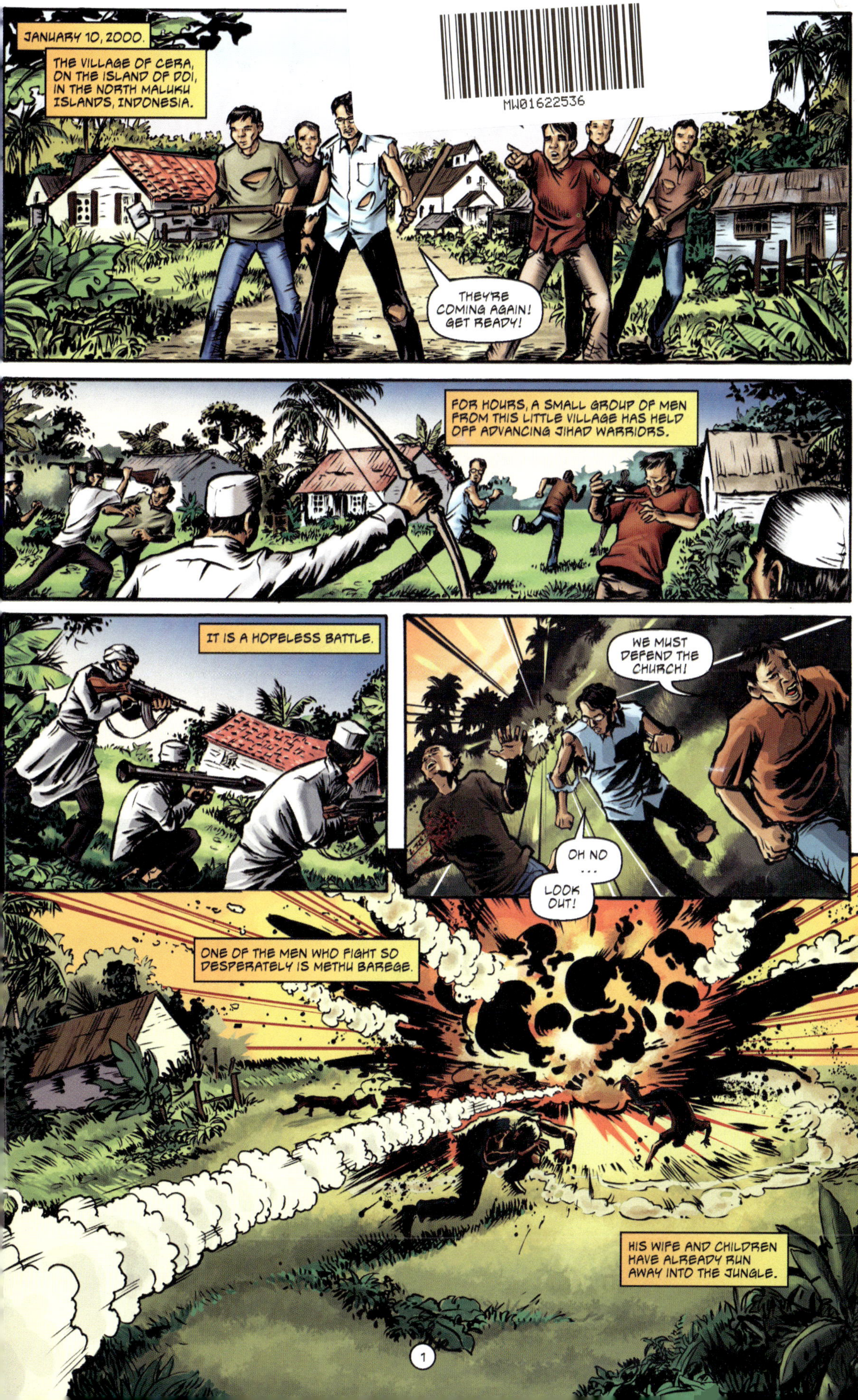

IT IS A HOPELESS BATTLE.

WE MUST DEFEND THE CHURCH!

OH NO . . .

LOOK OUT!

ONE OF THE MEN WHO FIGHT SO DESPERATELY IS METHU BAREGE.

HIS WIFE AND CHILDREN HAVE ALREADY RUN AWAY INTO THE JUNGLE.

METHU HAD EXPERIENCED SOME OF THE TENSIONS BETWEEN THE CHRISTIANS AND THE MUSLIMS IN THIS REGION OF INDONESIA.
NOTHING LIKE THIS, THOUGH.
THIS KIND OF VIOLENCE WOULD HAPPEN ON OTHER ISLANDS, MAYBE IN OTHER VILLAGES.
BUT NOT HERE IN HIS HOME, NOT TO HIM AND HIS FAMILY . . .
NOT LIKE THIS . . .
NO . . .
NO!!!

The Voice of the Martyrs
The Voice of the Martyrs presents
HOPE AMID HORROR
The true story of Methu and Adel
A Graphic Novella

The Voice of the Martyrs presents

HOPE AMID HORROR

The true story of Methu and Adel

The true story of Methu and Adel Barege and what happened in the village of Cera, on the island of Doi, in the North Maluku Islands, Indonesia, beginning on January 10, 2000.

Written by: **Ben Avery** Cover by: **Doug Klauba**
Art by: **Rob Woodrum** Editor: **Clash**

About The Voice of the Martyrs

The Voice of the Martyrs is a non-profit, inter-denominational Christian organization dedicated to assisting the persecuted church worldwide. VOM was founded in 1967 by Pastor Richard Wurmbrand, who was imprisoned 14 years in Communist Romania for his faith in Christ. His wife, Sabina, was imprisoned for three years. In the 1960s, Richard, Sabina, and their son, Mihai, were ransomed out of Romania and came to the United States. Throughout their lives, the Wurmbrands spread the message of the atrocities that Christians endure in restricted nations, while establishing a network of offices dedicated to assisting the persecuted church. The Voice of the Martyrs continues in this mission around the world today.

First printing: May 2010.

METHU!
CAN YOU RUN?
WE MUST RUN!
YES ... RUN ...

THERE IS NOTHING FOR US HERE ...

MUCH OF HIS VILLAGE DESTROYED, METHU FLEES.

FOR WHILE THERE MAY NOT BE ANYTHING FOR HIM IN THE VILLAGE ...

...THERE IS SOMETHING FOR HIM IN THE JUNGLE.
OH, METHU! THANK THE LORD!
ADEL! CHRISTINA! CHRISTIANO!
HURRY! WE MUST HIDE DEEPER IN THE JUNGLE!

I KNEW YOU'D FIND US!
OF COURSE! REMEMBER WHAT THE PASTOR SAID?
THE PASTOR! THAT HAD BEEN SO LONG AGO, IN ANOTHER WORLD, IT SEEMED ...

JULY 1989. ADEL'S HOME.
MOM, EVERY DAY HE COMES, AND EVERY DAY HE ASKS THE SAME QUESTION, AND EVERY DAY I GIVE HIM THE SAME ANSWER!
I DO NOT WANT TO MARRY HIM! HE LOOKS LIKE A MONKEY!
GET OUT THERE AND SHOW SOME RESPECT!
A MAN AS DETERMINED AS HE IS, HE WILL TAKE CARE OF YOU, ADEL.

ADEL, SINCE YOU STILL HAVE NOT ANSWERED ME, I WILL ASK YOU AGAIN.
WHAT DO YOU MEAN!?! I HAVE ANSWERED YOU! THE SAME ANSWER, EVERY TIME!!!
METHU, I'M TOO YOUNG TO GET MARRIED.
I DON'T WANT TO GET MARRIED, AND EVEN IF I DID, IT WOULD NOT BE TO YOU!

I UNDERSTAND. IF YOU DO NOT WANT TO ANSWER TODAY, I CAN WAIT UNTIL TOMORROW.
I'LL BE BACK TOMORROW, FOR I BELIEVE GOD HAS BROUGHT US TOGETHER.
MY FAITH GIVES ME HOPE THAT YOU AND I WILL BE MARRIED, ADEL, AND SOON.

EVEN IF I LOOK LIKE A MONKEY.

THREE MONTHS LATER.
METHU, ADEL, I PRONOUNCE YOU HUSBAND AND WIFE!
WHAT GOD HAS BROUGHT TOGETHER, LET NO MAN SEPARATE!
THE WEDDING IS TRADITIONAL, BEGINNING EARLY IN THE AFTERNOON, COMPLETE WITH TWO FULL MEALS FOR THE ENTIRE VILLAGE, AND GOING LONG INTO THE NIGHT.

THANK YOU, PASTOR.
YES! FOR EVERYTHING!
I KNOW YOU'RE WORRIED, MARRYING SO YOUNG. YOU MAY WONDER IF YOU'VE MADE A MISTAKE OVER THE COMING DAYS AND WEEKS AND MONTHS.
BUT YOU ARE NOW HUSBAND AND WIFE, AND I HAVE SEEN YOUR FAITH.
TRULY, ONLY GOD CAN SEPARATE YOU NOW ...

JANUARY 10, 2000.
TWO HOURS OF CRAWLING THROUGH THE TALL GRASS LATER . . .
METHU! THE CHILDREN . . . WE'RE ALL SO TIRED . . .
JUST A LITTLE MORE, ADEL.
LOOK!!!

COME! HURRY!
OH, THANK YOU LORD!

METHU, WHAT NOW?
THERE'S ONLY ONE THING WE CAN DO NOW . . .

DAWN. THE NEXT DAY.
MOMMY?
WHAT IS IT, CHRISTIANO?
I'M SO HUNGRY!

I'LL SEE WHAT FOOD I CAN FIND.
I'LL BE BACK SOON.

COMFORTING HER CHILDREN IN THE CHILL OF THE MORNING, ADEL KNOWS THERE IS NOTHING SHE CAN DO EXCEPT HAVE FAITH THAT GOD WILL TAKE CARE OF THEM.
BUT THAT WAS THE WAY IT WAS AT THE BEGINNING OF THEIR LIVES AS WELL. ADEL CANNOT HELP REMEMBERING . . .

ARE YOU SURE?
YES!
REMEMBERING THE JOY SHE AND METHU FELT WHEN, A MONTH AFTER THEIR WEDDING, THEY LEARNED SHE WAS PREGNANT!

REMEMBERING THE DESPAIR SHE AND METHU FELT WHEN, AFTER NINE MONTHS, THE CHILD WAS DELIVERED STILLBORN.

REMEMBERING THE FEAR WHEN, FIVE MONTHS LATER, ADEL WAS ONCE MORE PREGNANT.
ADEL, PREPARE YOURSELF. IF THIS BABY DIES AS WELL . . .

REMEMBERING THE FAITH SHE AND METHU FELT, EVEN THOUGH THE CHILD CAME THREE MONTHS EARLY.
OH, MY LITTLE CHRISTINA, YOU ARE SO, SO SMALL . . .
YOUR FATHER AND I LOVE YOU SO MUCH! WE KNOW GOD IS GOING TO PROTECT YOU!

REMEMBERING THE HOPE ADEL AND METHU FELT TWO YEARS LATER, AND NOW SHARED WITH THEIR DAUGHTER CHRISTINA.
HELLO, BABY!

REMEMBERING THE EXCITEMENT ADEL AND METHU FELT SOON AFTER CHRISTIANO WAS BORN, AS THEY MOVED OUT FROM METHU'S FAMILY'S HOUSE AND INTO THEIR OWN HOME . . .
IT'S A HUMBLE HOUSE. A SMALL HOUSE.
IT'S *OUR* HOUSE.

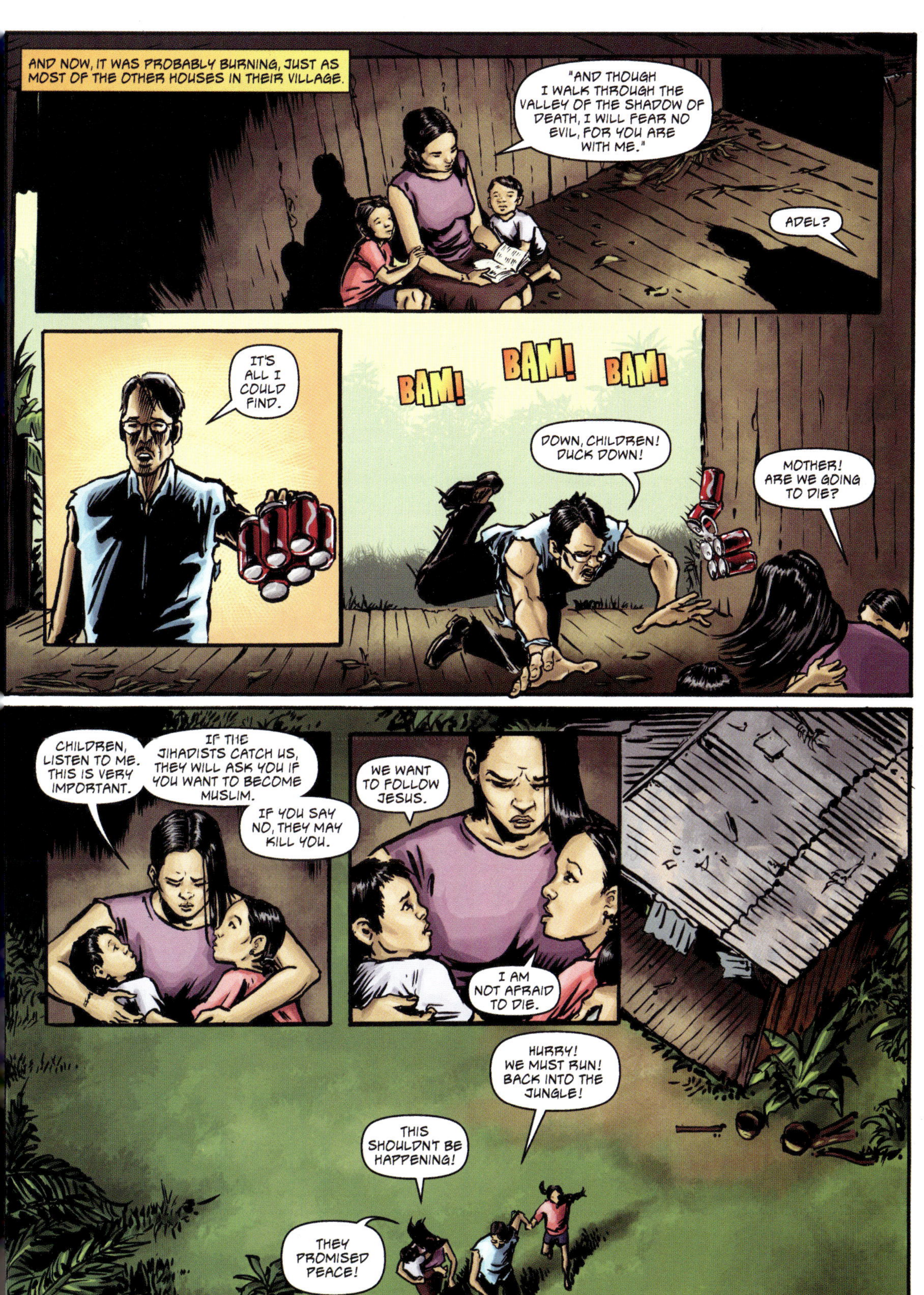
AND NOW, IT WAS PROBABLY BURNING, JUST AS MOST OF THE OTHER HOUSES IN THEIR VILLAGE.
"AND THOUGH I WALK THROUGH THE VALLEY OF THE SHADOW OF DEATH, I WILL FEAR NO EVIL, FOR YOU ARE WITH ME."
ADEL?
IT'S ALL I COULD FIND.
BAM! BAM! BAM!
DOWN, CHILDREN! DUCK DOWN!
MOTHER! ARE WE GOING TO DIE?
CHILDREN, LISTEN TO ME. THIS IS VERY IMPORTANT.
IF THE JIHADISTS CATCH US, THEY WILL ASK YOU IF YOU WANT TO BECOME MUSLIM.
IF YOU SAY NO, THEY MAY KILL YOU.
WE WANT TO FOLLOW JESUS.
I AM NOT AFRAID TO DIE.
HURRY! WE MUST RUN! BACK INTO THE JUNGLE!
THIS SHOULDN'T BE HAPPENING!
THEY PROMISED PEACE!
ALTHOUGH THE ATTACK OCCURRED JUST HOURS BEFORE, ADEL'S THOUGHTS TRAVEL BACK FOUR MONTHS EARLIER, TO THE TRUE BEGINNING OF THIS NIGHTMARE.

SEPTEMBER 9, 1999.
FOR A WHILE, A RUMOR HAD GONE AROUND SAYING THAT THE 9TH DAY OF THE 9TH MONTH IN 1999 WOULD BE A DARK DAY FOR THE CHRISTIANS ON THEIR ISLAND.
WHAT'S GOING ON?
SOME SORT OF PEACE RALLY.
IT'S THE MUSLIMS!
LOVE AND PEACE
THE RUMOR MUST HAVE BEEN JUST THAT: A RUMOR.
WE SHOULD COMMIT TO PEACE!
THERE SHOULD NOT BE VIOLENCE BETWEEN THE VILLAGES OF THE MUSLIMS AND THE VILLAGES OF THE CHRISTIANS!
AND FOR FOUR MONTHS, THERE WAS PEACE.

UNTIL THE MORNING OF JANUARY 10, 2000.
WHAT'S GOING ON?
THE MUSLIMS! THEY'RE COMING! IT'S JIHAD!
THEY'RE ARMED!

CHRISTINA! CHRISTIANO!
COME HERE! COME HERE!

NOW HURRY!
WE MUST FLEE!

IT'S OKAY. FATHER WILL BE BACK SOON.
WITH FOOD?
WITH FOOD.
NOW, LISTEN, "THE LORD IS MY SHEPHERD --"
RAT -A- TAT RAT -A- TAT
RUN! ADEL! RUN! GET THE CHILDREN AWAY!
RAT -A- TAT
METHU !?!
BACK INTO THE JUNGLE! RUN!!!
OOOOF!

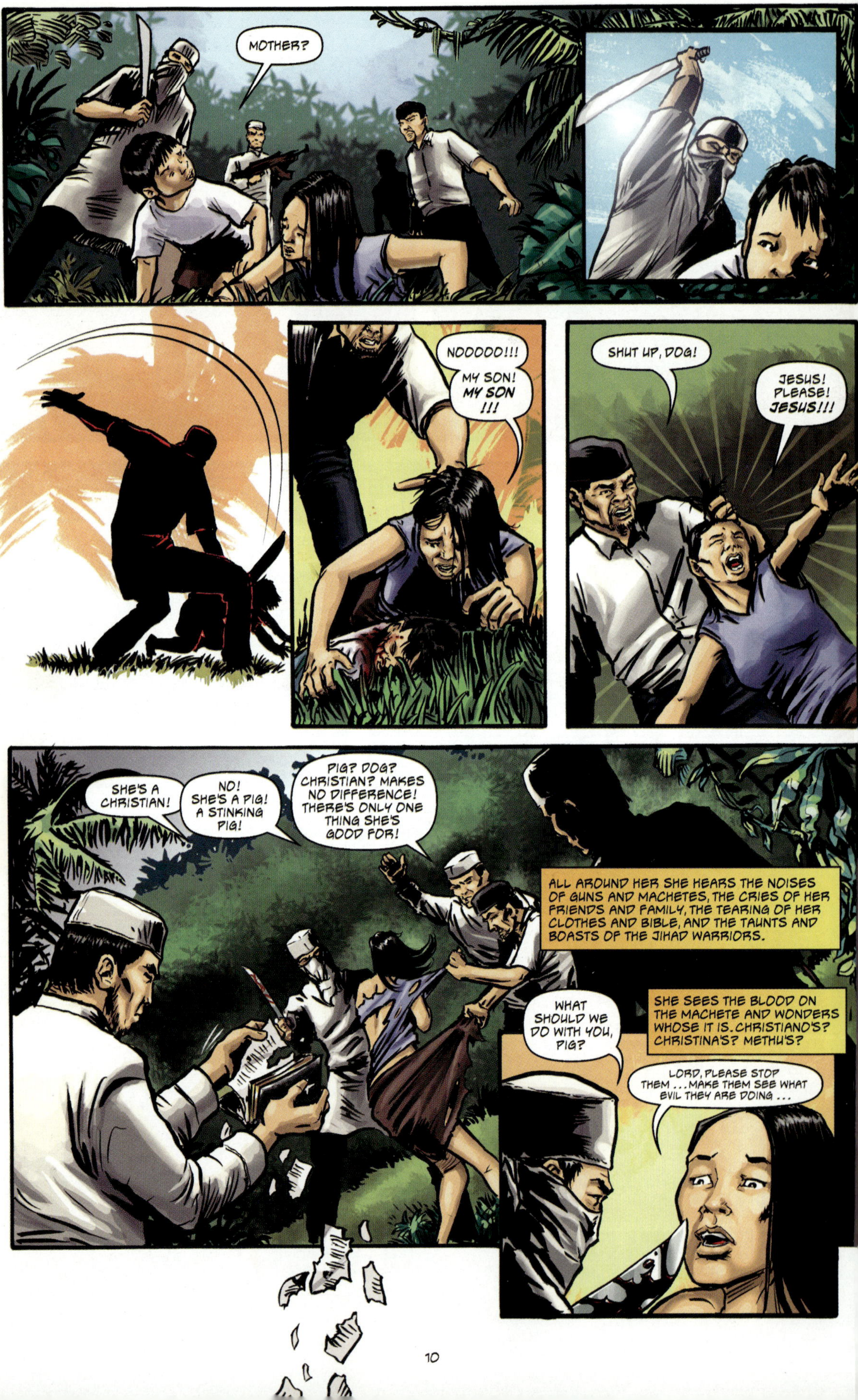

SHE'S A CHRISTIAN!

NO! SHE'S A PIG! A STINKING PIG!

PIG? DOG? CHRISTIAN? MAKES NO DIFFERENCE! THERE'S ONLY ONE THING SHE'S GOOD FOR!

ALL AROUND HER SHE HEARS THE NOISES OF GUNS AND MACHETES, THE CRIES OF HER FRIENDS AND FAMILY, THE TEARING OF HER CLOTHES AND BIBLE, AND THE TAUNTS AND BOASTS OF THE JIHAD WARRIORS.

WHAT SHOULD WE DO WITH YOU, PIG?

SHE SEES THE BLOOD ON THE MACHETE AND WONDERS WHOSE IT IS. CHRISTIANO'S? CHRISTINA'S? METHU'S?

LORD, PLEASE STOP THEM . . . MAKE THEM SEE WHAT EVIL THEY ARE DOING . . .

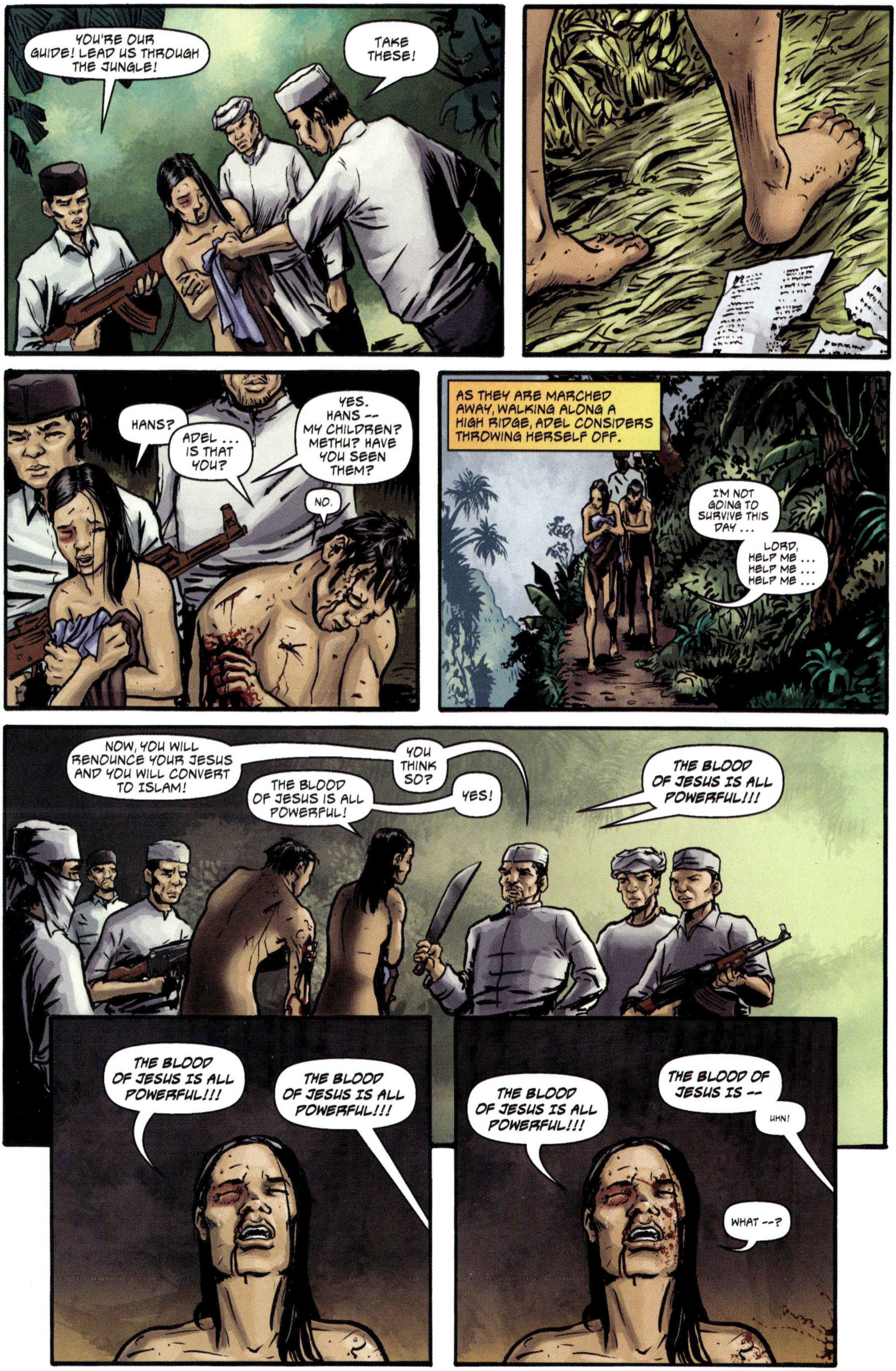

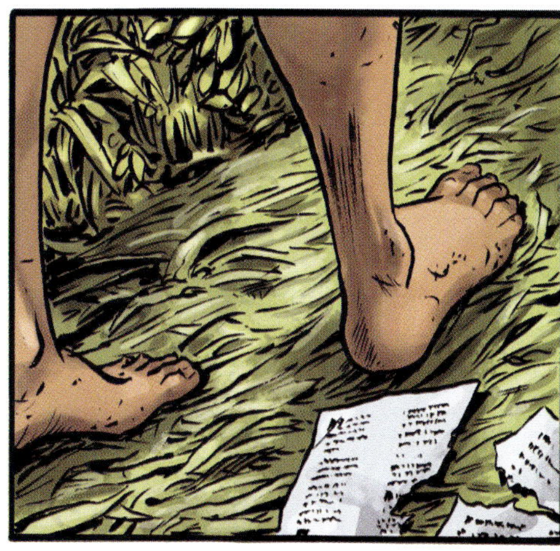

NOW, YOU WILL RENOUNCE YOUR JESUS AND YOU WILL CONVERT TO ISLAM!

THE BLOOD OF JESUS IS ALL POWERFUL!

YOU THINK SO?

YES!

THE BLOOD OF JESUS IS ALL POWERFUL!!!

THE BLOOD OF JESUS IS ALL POWERFUL!!!

THE BLOOD OF JESUS IS ALL POWERFUL!!!

THE BLOOD OF JESUS IS ALL POWERFUL!!!

THE BLOOD OF JESUS IS --

UHN!

WHAT --?

WHAT DID YOU DO!?!
WHAT HAVE YOU DONE TO HIM!?!
HOW COULD ANYONE DO THAT TO ANOTHER PERSON!?!

NOTHING COMPARED TO WHAT WE'RE GOING TO DO TO YOU!
THE BLOOD OF JESUS IS --
-- ALL POWERFUL ...

SOMEHOW, EVEN AS HER BODY IS BRUISED AND BATTERED BY THE BEATINGS THE MEN GIVE HER, ADEL'S COURAGE RISES.
THE BLOOD --
NNNG!
-- OF JESUS --
UHN!
-- IS ALL --
OOOF!
-- POWERFUL!
SHE HAD EXPECTED TO DIE AT THEIR HANDS, AND YET HER BODY STILL LIVES!

SHUT THIS INFIDEL UP!
GLADLY!
THE BLOOD OF JESUS IS ... ALL ... POWERFUL ...

YOU WILL BE SILENT!

THE PIG WON'T SQUEAL ANYMORE!
PTOO!
THE BLOOD OF JESUS IS ALL POWERFUL.
BRACING HERSELF FOR MORE BEATINGS, ADEL'S BODY GROWS WEAKER ...
THE BLOOD OF JESUS IS ALL POWERFUL!
... BUT NOT HER SPIRIT.

IN THE DARKNESS, IT IS HARD TO SEE THE DETAILS OF THE BODIES. BUT METHU EASILY IDENTIFIES THE ONE SMALL BODY WITH A NEARLY SEVERED HEAD . . .

AND NEAR SOME OF THE BODIES, THE TORN, BURNED REMAINS OF A BIBLE.

ADEL'S BIBLE.

LEAVING THAT CARNAGE BEHIND, METHU CONTINUES HIS SEARCH FOR HIS WIFE AND DAUGHTER . . .

. . . ONLY TO FIND MORE DEATH AND DESTRUCTION.

METHU, WE WILL DIE IF WE STAY HERE.

I CAN ONLY HOPE THEY'VE BEEN CAPTURED, NOT KILLED . . .

AND SO, METHU LEAVES, SEEKING REFUGE ON THE LARGER ISLAND OF HALMAHERA.

THE NEXT DAY, ADEL'S BEATINGS ARE REPLACED BY INTERROGATIONS:

WHERE ARE THE CHRISTIANS HIDING?

I RECOGNIZE YOU. YOU CAME TO OUR VILLAGE, PREACHING PEACE!

ANSWER ME!

ADEL KNOWS THE ANSWER. AND SHE ALSO KNOWS THAT IF SHE GIVES THIS MAN THE ANSWER, SHE WILL GIVE HIM METHU AS WELL.

I WILL DIE FIRST.

YOU WILL TELL US WHERE THEY ARE!

AND SO THE INTERROGATION CONTINUES. ELEVEN MEN ARE ASSIGNED TO INTERROGATE HER.

WE JUST WANT TO KNOW WHERE THEY ARE, AND THEN YOU CAN GO HOME.

...WE WON'T HURT THEM.

YOU WANT TO GO HOME, YES?

YOU WILL EAT!

SPIT IT OUT, AND I WILL FORCE IT IN AGAIN!

BUT WHILE SHE HAS NOT EATEN IN THREE DAYS, ADEL REFUSES.

WORD OF HER REFUSAL TO SPEAK OR EAT OR COOPERATE IN ANY WAY TRAVELS FAST.

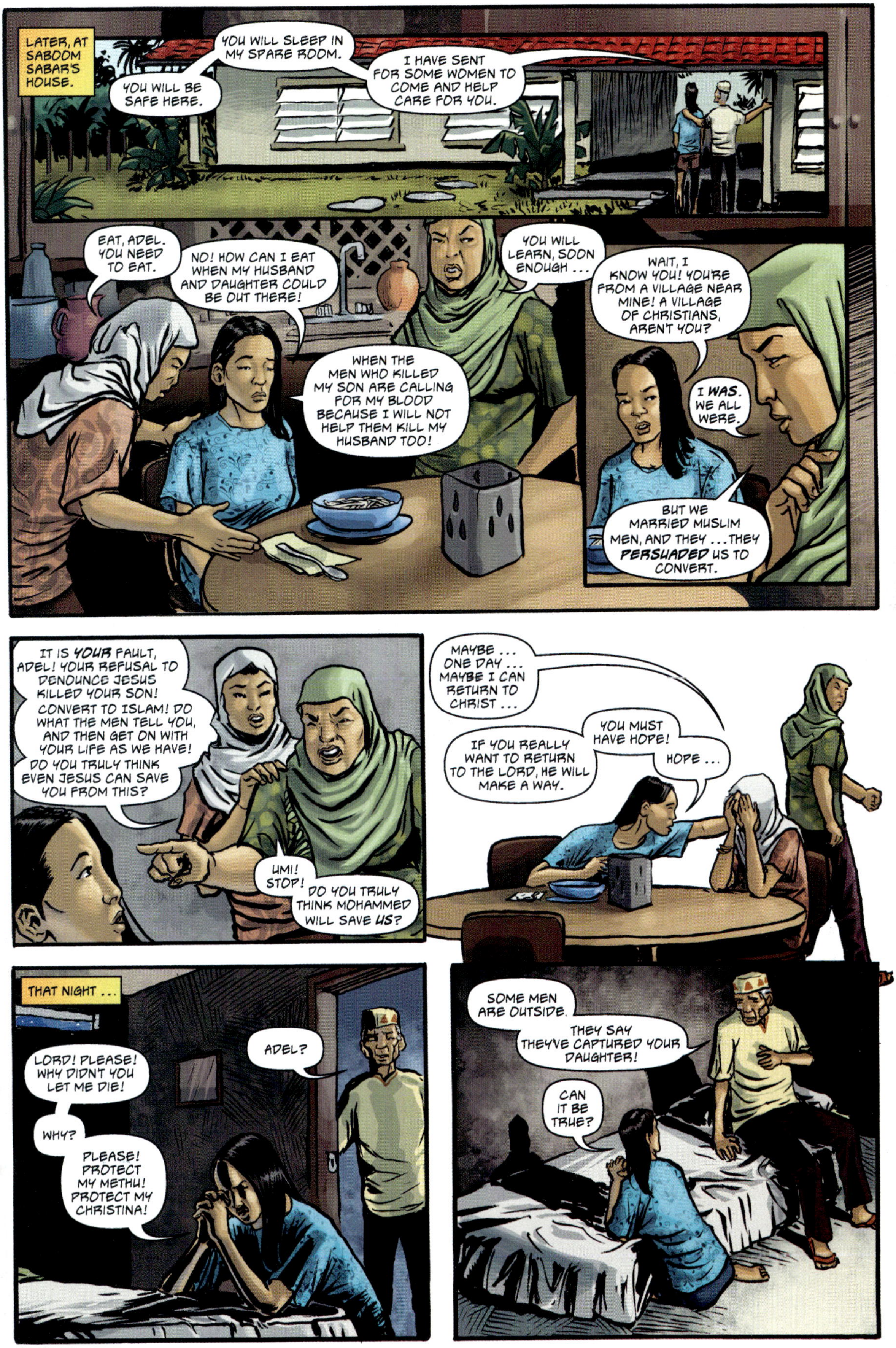

LATER, AT SABOOM SABAR'S HOUSE.

YOU WILL BE SAFE HERE.

YOU WILL SLEEP IN MY SPARE ROOM.

I HAVE SENT FOR SOME WOMEN TO COME AND HELP CARE FOR YOU.

EAT, ADEL. YOU NEED TO EAT.

NO! HOW CAN I EAT WHEN MY HUSBAND AND DAUGHTER COULD BE OUT THERE!

WHEN THE MEN WHO KILLED MY SON ARE CALLING FOR MY BLOOD BECAUSE I WILL NOT HELP THEM KILL MY HUSBAND TOO!

YOU WILL LEARN, SOON ENOUGH ...

WAIT, I KNOW YOU! YOU'RE FROM A VILLAGE NEAR MINE! A VILLAGE OF CHRISTIANS, AREN'T YOU?

I ***WAS***. WE ALL WERE.

BUT WE MARRIED MUSLIM MEN, AND THEY ... THEY ***PERSUADED*** US TO CONVERT.

SABOOM SABAR ACCOMPANIES ADEL TO THE VILLAGE OF SALUBI.
THE RECEPTION IS FAR FROM WARM ...

INFIDEL! COME TO SEE YOUR FOUL OFFSPRING!
NO! PLEASE! STOP!
THERE'S NO NEED FOR THIS!

COMING HERE WAS A MISTAKE, FOR NOW YOU WILL BE HOSTAGE JUST AS YOUR DAUGHTER IS!
THIS IS THE LAST TIME I WILL BE ABLE TO PROTECT YOU! THEY WILL KILL ME TOO!

CHRISTINA!
MAMA!!!

MOMMY! THEY KILLED GRANDMAMMA! AND CHRISTIANO! I SAW HIM!
OH, CHRISTINA! I KNOW, CHILD, I KNOW ... BUT WE'RE TOGETHER NOW!

TWO MONTHS AFTER THE ATTACK.
IT IS TIME.
WE HAVEN'T HEARD FROM ANY SURVIVORS! WHAT MAKES YOU THINK THERE ARE ANY?
I MUST FIND OUT IF ADEL AND CHRISTINA ARE ALIVE!
THE MUSLIM JIHADISTS RUN THE ISLAND!
I AM WILLING TO TAKE THE RISK TO SEE MY FAMILY! ARE YOU?

METHU DOES NOT KNOW WHAT TO EXPECT, BUT HE HAS HOPE.

STATE YOUR BUSINESS!
THIS PLACE IS MY HOME!
CHRISTIANS, EH? COME TO CONVERT?
NO! I DID NOT COME HERE TO CONVERT!

YOU **WILL** CONVERT TO ISLAM, NOW, OR YOU **WILL** DIE!
I AM LOOKING FOR MY WIFE! MY DAUGHTER!

OH, YOU WILL CONVERT. TRUST ME!
NEVER! I'LL NEV--
ADEL?
I CAN'T BELIEVE IT! IT'S HER!

THANK YOU, JESUS! YOU HAVE PRESERVED MY WIFE AND DAUGHTER!

MOVE, PIG!
OH, JESUS PLEASE HELP US! HELP US ALL!
YOU'LL BE SINGING A DIFFERENT TUNE SOON ENOUGH!

SOON AFTER ...
SO, YOU ARE HERE TO FIND YOUR WIFE AND DAUGHTER?
I HEAR YOU SAW THEM WHEN YOU WERE ON THE DOCK.
WELL, IF YOU WANT TO SEE THEM AGAIN, YOU WILL CONVERT.
NO. NEVER.
THINK THIS THROUGH.
IF YOU DO NOT TURN AWAY FROM THE LICE-INFESTED, LONG HAIRED PIG YOU CALL JESUS, NOT ONLY WILL YOU DIE, BUT YOUR FAMILY WILL AS WELL.

BUT IF YOU DO CONVERT, WE WILL GIVE YOU MONEY AND PROPERTY AND ALLOW YOU TO LIVE HERE AS A MUSLIM!
YOU CAN OFFER ME A PILE OF GOLD AS TALL AS I AM! I WILL NOT DO IT!
NONE OF US WILL!

BAH! YOU ARE ALL FOOLS!
YOU HAVE THIRTY MINUTES TO DECIDE!

METHU, WHAT ARE WE GOING TO DO?
REMEMBER WHAT JESUS SAYS IN MATTHEW: "WHOEVER DENIES ME BEFORE MEN, HIM I WILL DENY BEFORE MY FATHER WHO IS IN HEAVEN."
I NEVER WANT TO BE DISOWNED BY JESUS.
THEN WHEN THEY RETURN WE WILL TELL THEM.
AFTER THIRTY MINUTES ...
COME!
WE WILL NOT --
SHUT UP!
WE ARE TAKING YOU TO SEE YOUR WIFE!

I AM TAKING ADEL AND CHRISTINA! THEY WILL MEET WITH ADEL'S CHRISTIAN HUSBAND!
THEY WILL BE ASKED IF THEY WISH TO STAY HERE OR IF THEY WOULD LIKE TO GO BACK WITH HER PIG HUSBAND METHU!
WHAT? METHU? NOW?
IF EITHER ONE OF THEM SAYS THEY WISH TO GO WITH METHU, WE WILL KILL EVERY SINGLE ONE OF YOU!
EVERY.
SINGLE.
ONE.

COME. NOW.
ADEL IS QUICKLY TRANSPORTED TO DAHMA, WHERE THE MEETING WILL TAKE PLACE.

YOU WILL BE ASKED THIS EXACT QUESTION: "DO YOU WANT TO LEAVE WITH METHU OR REMAIN IN SALUBI?"
YOU BOTH KNOW THE ANSWER YOU ARE TO GIVE.
GOVERNMENT OFFICIALS WILL RECORD YOUR ANSWERS, WHICH WILL BE USED TO PROVE NO ONE IS BEING HELD AGAINST THEIR WILL.

AFTER YOUR OFFICIAL ANSWER, YOU WILL BE GIVEN FIVE MINUTES ALONE, DURING WHICH TIME YOU WILL NOT WHISPER.
AND THEN, WE WILL HONOR YOUR WISHES --
-- AND TAKE YOU BACK TO SALUBI, JUST AS YOU INSTRUCTED US.

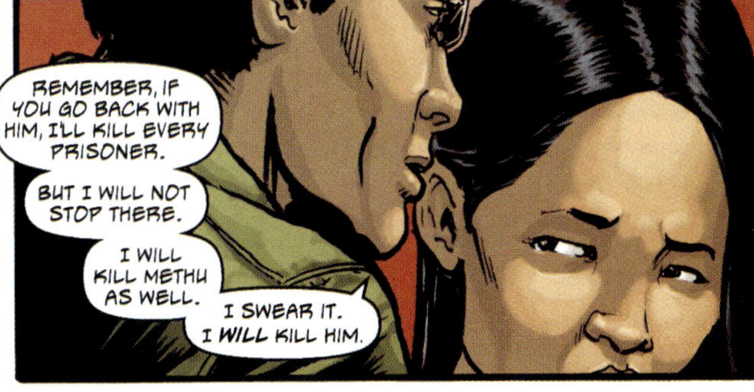
REMEMBER, IF YOU GO BACK WITH HIM, I'LL KILL EVERY PRISONER.
BUT I WILL NOT STOP THERE.
I WILL KILL METHU AS WELL.
I SWEAR IT. I **WILL** KILL HIM.

ADEL! CHRISTINA!
METHU!
DADDY!
SIT DOWN.

ADEL, DO YOU WANT TO LEAVE WITH METHU OR REMAIN IN SALUBI?
I --
ADEL! DO YOU WANT TO LEAVE WITH YOUR HUSBAND OR REMAIN IN SALUBI?

METHU, I . . . I CANNOT GO WITH YOU.

CHRISTINA! DO YOU WISH TO LEAVE WITH YOUR FATHER OR REMAIN IN SALUBI?
I CAN'T, DADDY! I CAN'T GO WITH YOU!
I'M SO SORRY! I WANT --
ENOUGH!

WE ARE FINISHED HERE!
THE RECORD WILL STATE YOUR DESIRE TO STAY.
NOT ANOTHER WORD ABOUT IT! YOU HAVE FIVE MINUTES!

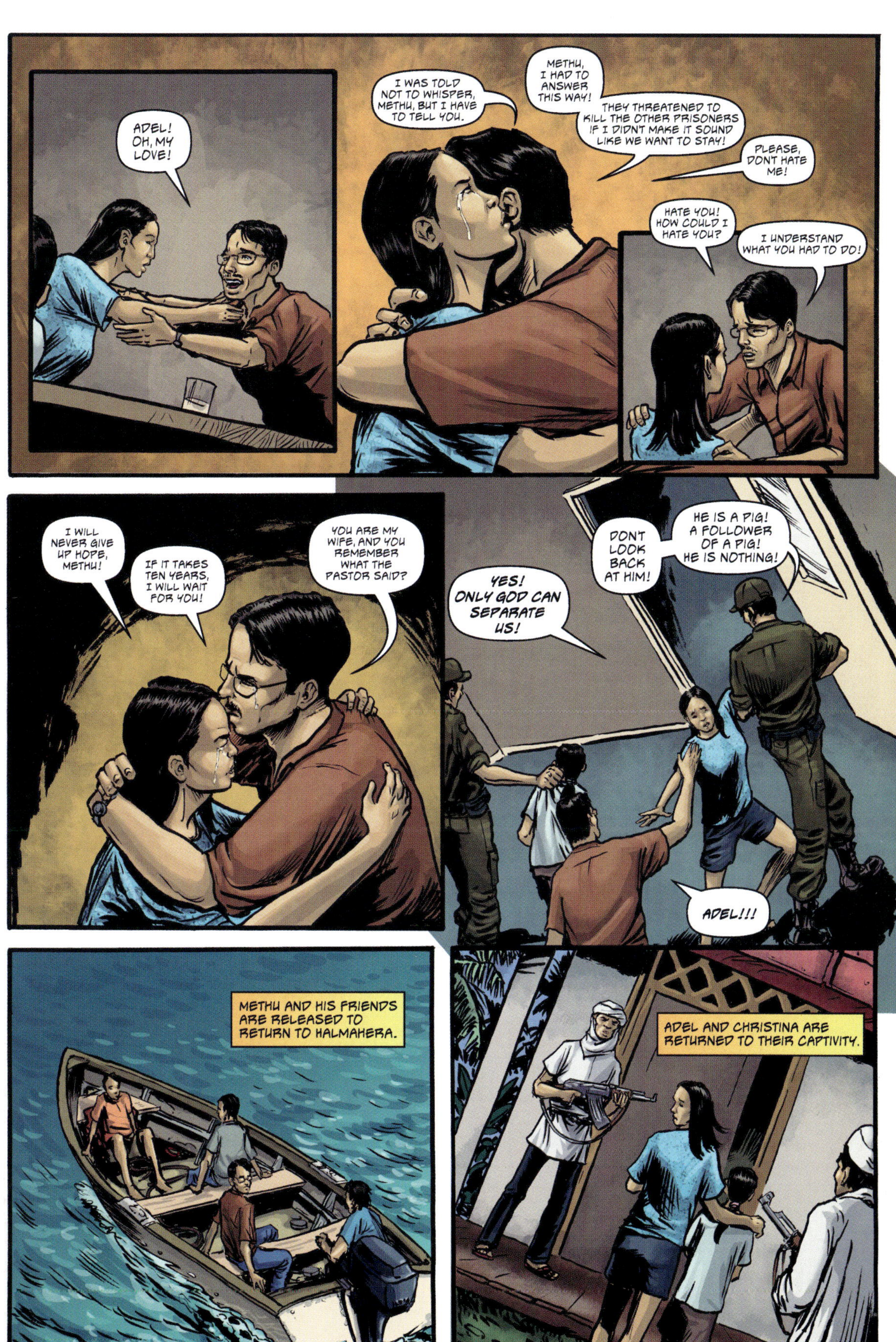
ADEL! OH, MY LOVE!
I WAS TOLD NOT TO WHISPER, METHU, BUT I HAVE TO TELL YOU.
METHU, I HAD TO ANSWER THIS WAY!
THEY THREATENED TO KILL THE OTHER PRISONERS IF I DIDN'T MAKE IT SOUND LIKE WE WANT TO STAY!
PLEASE, DON'T HATE ME!
HATE YOU! HOW COULD I HATE YOU?
I UNDERSTAND WHAT YOU HAD TO DO!
I WILL NEVER GIVE UP HOPE, METHU!
IF IT TAKES TEN YEARS, I WILL WAIT FOR YOU!
YOU ARE MY WIFE, AND YOU REMEMBER WHAT THE PASTOR SAID?
YES! ONLY GOD CAN SEPARATE US!
DON'T LOOK BACK AT HIM!
HE IS A PIG! A FOLLOWER OF A PIG! HE IS NOTHING!
ADEL!!!
METHU AND HIS FRIENDS ARE RELEASED TO RETURN TO HALMAHERA.
ADEL AND CHRISTINA ARE RETURNED TO THEIR CAPTIVITY.

APRIL 10, 2000.
HOPE. IN THE DAYS, THE WEEKS, THE MONTHS FOLLOWING HER REUNION WITH METHU, SHE CLUNG TO THE HOPE THAT THEY WOULD BE TOGETHER AGAIN.
AND THEN . . .
NO!!!
NO! I CANNOT MARRY SOMEONE ELSE!
I AM MARRIED TO METHU!

METHU IS NOT A MAN, HE IS A PIG, AND I DO NOT RECOGNIZE YOUR MARRIAGE TO HIM!
IF YOU DO NOT MARRY THIS ONE MAN, I WILL LET ALL OF MY MEN HAVE YOU!
NOW, MEET ALMIN! YOUR NEW HUSBAND!

SLOWLY, ADEL'S HOPE DIES, AS SHE IS FORCED TO MOVE IN WITH ALMIN.
FORCED TO SHARE HIS HOME AS HIS WIFE, AND ALL OF WHAT THAT MEANS.

AND A FEW MONTHS LATER . . .
MOMMY? WHAT'S WRONG?
I'VE FEARED THIS MOMENT FROM THE TIME THEY TOLD ME I WAS TO BE "MARRIED" . . . I'M --

-- PREGNANT!
AS ADEL'S HOPE DIES, HER HATRED GROWS.
THEY KILLED HER SON. HER MOTHER.

THEY BEAT HER MERCILESSLY, COUNTLESS TIMES.
THEY TOOK AWAY HER CHANCE OF EVER BEING WITH METHU AGAIN.
AND THEY TOOK AWAY THE SANCTITY OF HER MARRIAGE WITH HIM.
THE CHILD THAT ALMIN HAD GIVEN HER WAS JUST A REMINDER OF ALL THAT HAD BEEN TAKEN AWAY FROM HER.
GOD HAD SAVED HER, BUT SAVED HER SO SHE COULD LIVE THIS LIFE?
MOM!

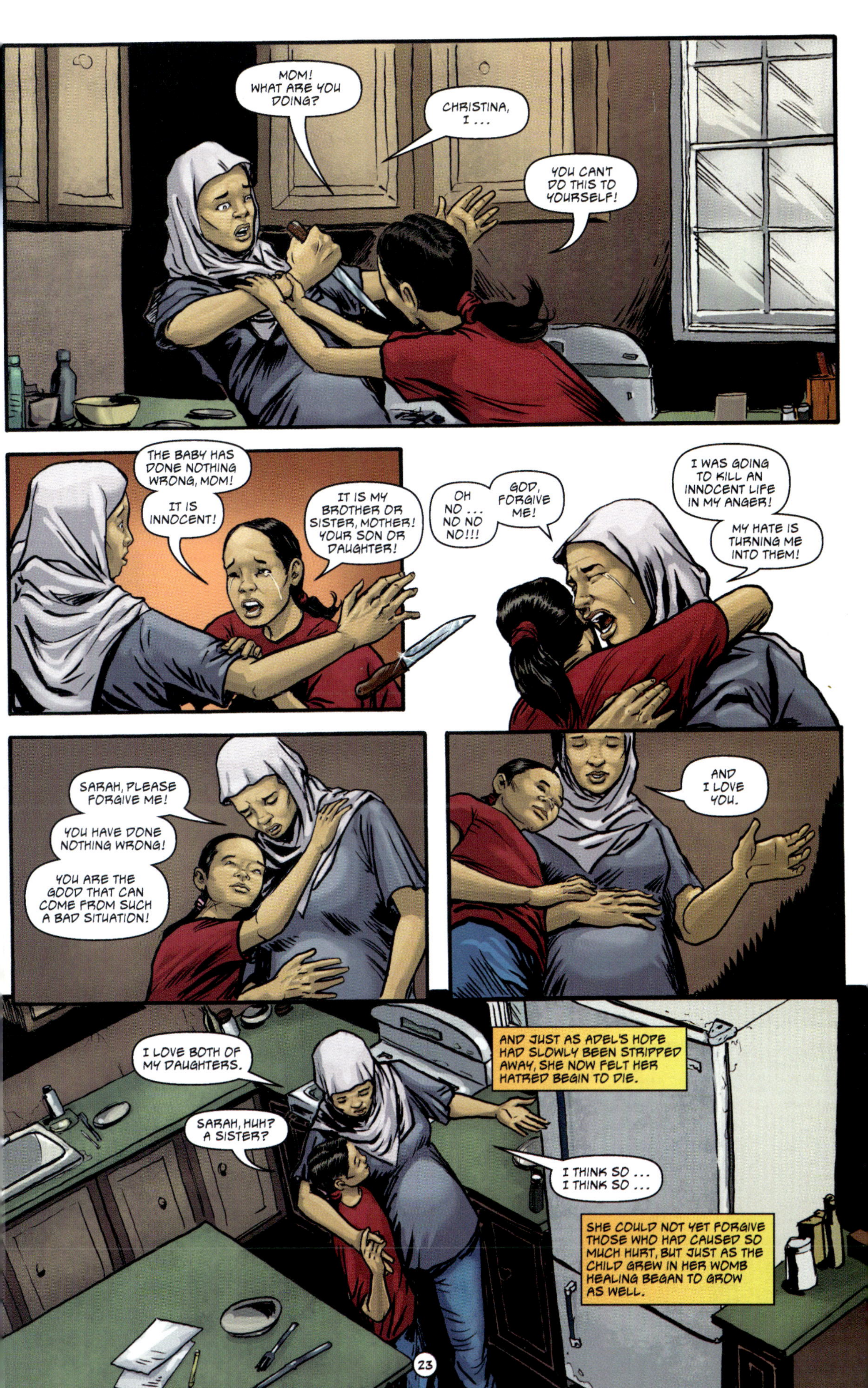
MOM! WHAT ARE YOU DOING?
CHRISTINA, I . . .
YOU CAN'T DO THIS TO YOURSELF!
THE BABY HAS DONE NOTHING WRONG, MOM!
IT IS INNOCENT!
IT IS MY BROTHER OR SISTER, MOTHER! YOUR SON OR DAUGHTER!
OH NO . . . NO NO NO!!!
GOD, FORGIVE ME!
I WAS GOING TO KILL AN INNOCENT LIFE IN MY ANGER!
MY HATE IS TURNING ME INTO THEM!
SARAH, PLEASE FORGIVE ME!
YOU HAVE DONE NOTHING WRONG!
YOU ARE THE GOOD THAT CAN COME FROM SUCH A BAD SITUATION!
AND I LOVE YOU.
AND JUST AS ADEL'S HOPE HAD SLOWLY BEEN STRIPPED AWAY, SHE NOW FELT HER HATRED BEGIN TO DIE.
I LOVE BOTH OF MY DAUGHTERS.
SARAH, HUH? A SISTER?
I THINK SO . . . I THINK SO . . .
SHE COULD NOT YET FORGIVE THOSE WHO HAD CAUSED SO MUCH HURT, BUT JUST AS THE CHILD GREW IN HER WOMB HEALING BEGAN TO GROW AS WELL.

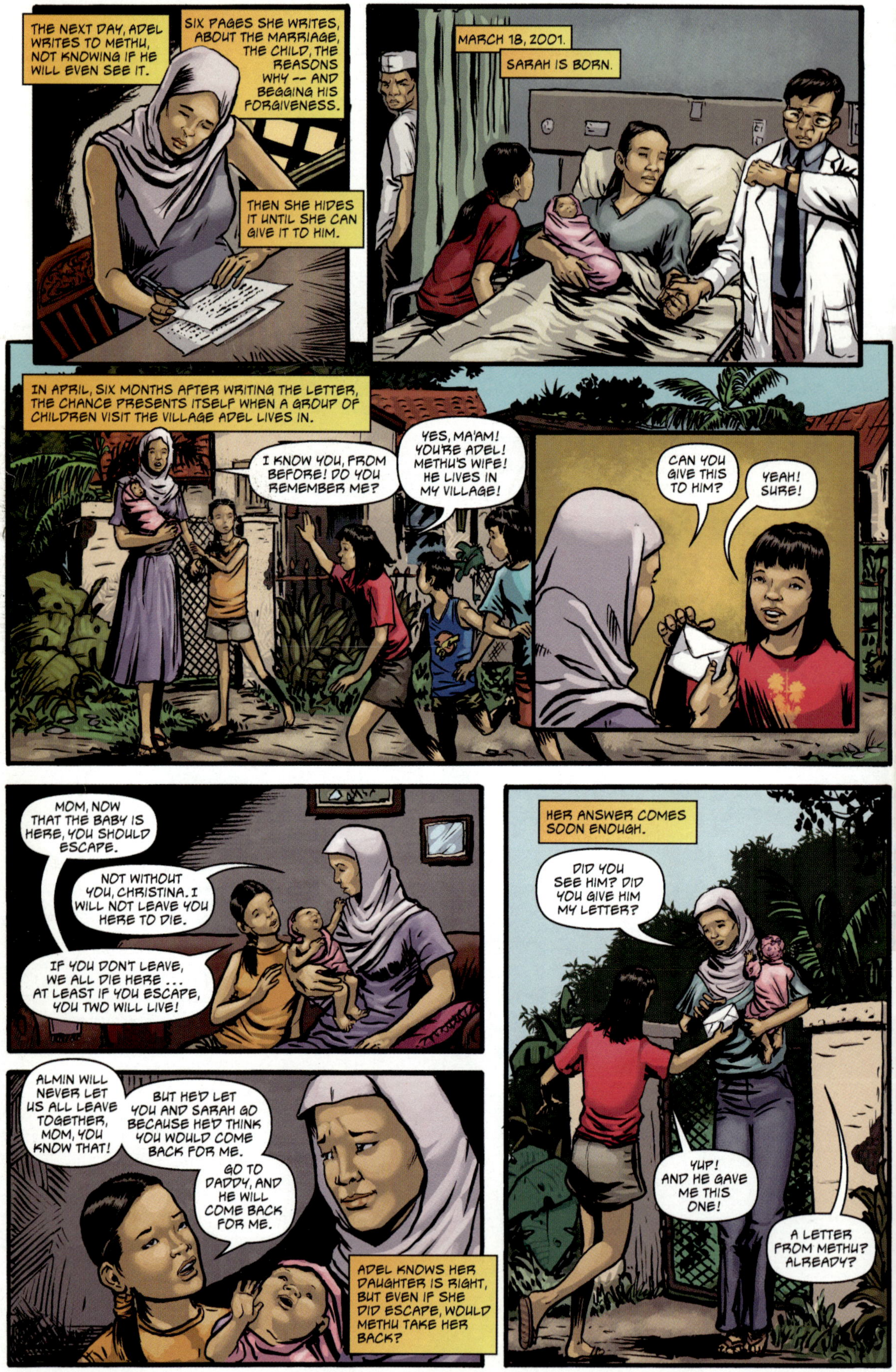

THE NEXT DAY, ADEL WRITES TO METHU, NOT KNOWING IF HE WILL EVEN SEE IT.

SIX PAGES SHE WRITES, ABOUT THE MARRIAGE, THE CHILD, THE REASONS WHY -- AND BEGGING HIS FORGIVENESS.

THEN SHE HIDES IT UNTIL SHE CAN GIVE IT TO HIM.

MARCH 18, 2001.

SARAH IS BORN.

IN APRIL, SIX MONTHS AFTER WRITING THE LETTER, THE CHANCE PRESENTS ITSELF WHEN A GROUP OF CHILDREN VISIT THE VILLAGE ADEL LIVES IN.

I KNOW YOU, FROM BEFORE! DO YOU REMEMBER ME?

YES, MA'AM! YOU'RE ADEL! METHU'S WIFE! HE LIVES IN MY VILLAGE!

CAN YOU GIVE THIS TO HIM?

YEAH! SURE!

DID HE HATE HER? HAD HE MARRIED ANOTHER WOMAN?

"ADEL, YOU COULD HAVE TEN CHILDREN BY TEN MEN, AND YOU WOULD STILL BE MY WIFE. DON'T YOU REMEMBER WHAT THE PASTOR TOLD YOU?

"ONLY GOD CAN SEPARATE US NOW. I LOVE YOU, METHU."

WITH A RENEWED HOPE, ADEL SETS INTO MOTION A DANGEROUS PLAN.

JUNE 18. ALMIN GIVES ADEL PERMISSION TO VISIT SOME RELATIVES ON A NEARBY ISLAND.

COME, CHRISTINA.

NO! SHE STAYS WITH ME.

BUT SHE SHOULD COME AS WELL!

NO! YOU WILL RUN IF YOUR DAUGHTER GOES ALONG.

IT'S OKAY, MOM.

PROMISE ME YOU'LL GO BACK TO DADDY! PROMISE YOU'LL ESCAPE!

I WILL BE OKAY! JESUS IS WITH ME!

ADEL WONDERS HOW SUCH A YOUNG GIRL COULD HAVE SUCH COURAGE AND FAITH.

SHE DECIDES TOO LATE!
ADEL !!!

AND THIS IS OUR NEW DAUGHTER?
SARAH.
SARAH!

BUT CHRISTINA! WHERE IS SHE?
WHY ?!?
I...I LEFT HER BEHIND ...

SHE BEGGED ME TO ESCAPE.
TO COME FIND YOU.
I SHOULDN'T HAVE ...

NO! ADEL, YOU DID THE RIGHT THING!
YOU KNOW WHERE SHE IS, AND I CAN FIND HER. I CAN RESCUE HER.
I WILL RESCUE HER!
JUST AS SHE SAID ...

METHU DOES NOT WASTE ANY TIME. IMMEDIATELY, HE GETS ALL THE INFORMATION HE CAN FROM HIS WIFE AND THEN HE SETS OUT.
COME BACK QUICKLY.
I WILL DO MY BEST.

METHU BIDES HIS TIME, WAITING FOR THE RIGHT OPPORTUNITY.
LORD, HELP ME.
I KNOW YOU WILL PROVIDE THE RIGHT MOMENT.
PLEASE, GUIDE ME. SHOW ME WHAT TO DO!

ADEL BIDES HER TIME AS WELL, WAITING FOR HER HUSBAND TO RETURN.
LORD, YOUR WORD SAYS I CAN DO ALL THINGS THROUGH YOU, BECAUSE YOU GIVE ME STRENGTH.
GIVE ME STRENGTH AS I WAIT FOR METHU, AND GIVE HIM STRENGTH TO DO WHAT IS REQUIRED OF HIM.

TWO WEEKS PASS, BUT ALMIN KEEPS CHRISTINA CLOSE TO HIM.
FOR HE KNOWS THAT CHRISTINA IS THE ONLY THING THAT WILL BRING ADEL -- AND HIS CHILD SARAH -- BACK.

FOR TWO WEEKS, METHU PRAYS FOR THE PERFECT MOMENT.
WHAT ARE YOU DOING, ALMIN?
THEY'RE HOLDING A CHRISTIAN AND MUSLIM RECONCILIATION MEETING IN DAHMA.
I MUST GO, AND THEREFORE YOU MUST COME AS WELL!
UNTIL, FINALLY...

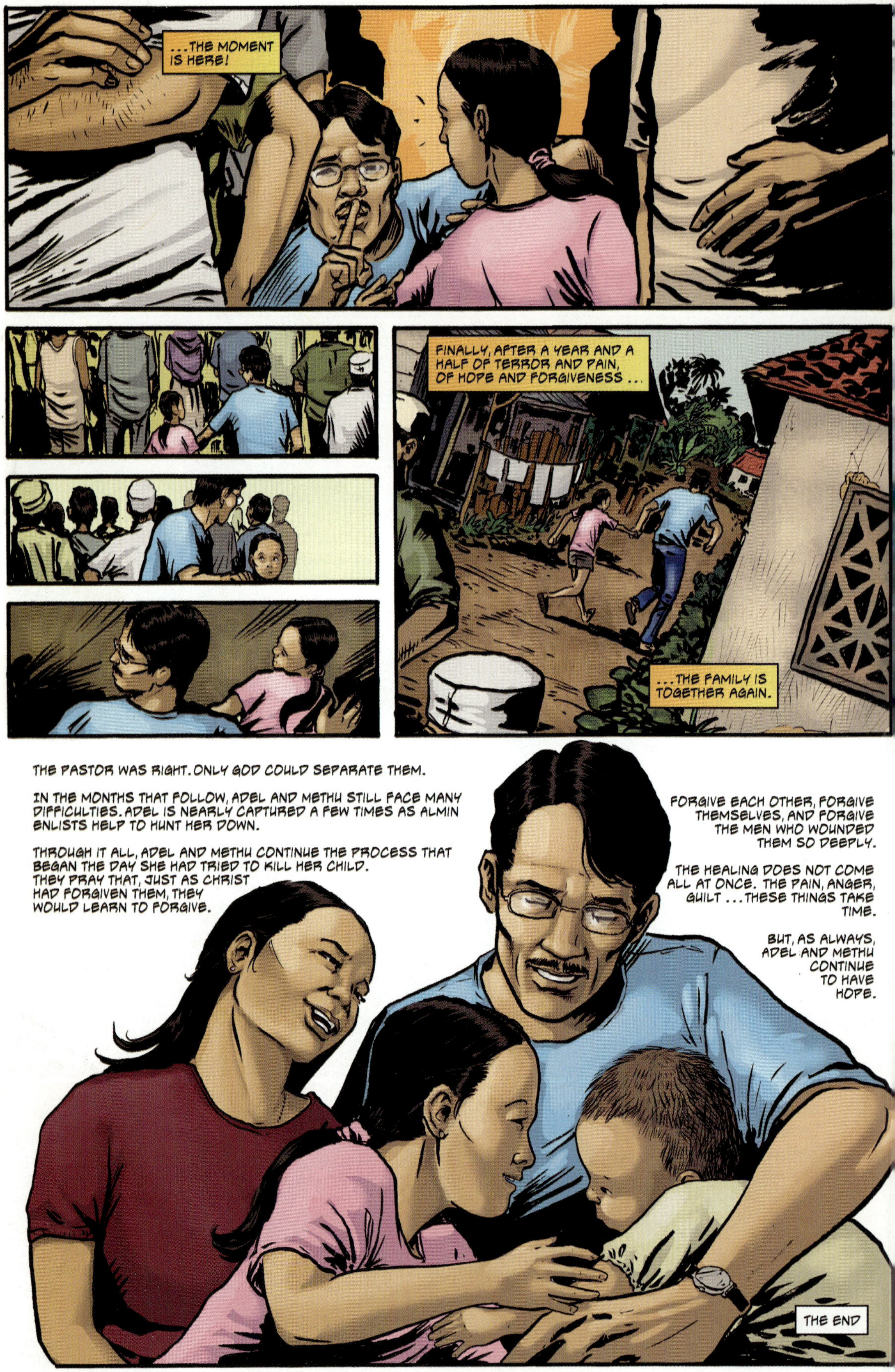

THE PASTOR WAS RIGHT. ONLY GOD COULD SEPARATE THEM.

IN THE MONTHS THAT FOLLOW, ADEL AND METHU STILL FACE MANY DIFFICULTIES. ADEL IS NEARLY CAPTURED A FEW TIMES AS ALMIN ENLISTS HELP TO HUNT HER DOWN.

THROUGH IT ALL, ADEL AND METHU CONTINUE THE PROCESS THAT BEGAN THE DAY SHE HAD TRIED TO KILL HER CHILD. THEY PRAY THAT, JUST AS CHRIST HAD FORGIVEN THEM, THEY WOULD LEARN TO FORGIVE.

FORGIVE EACH OTHER, FORGIVE THEMSELVES, AND FORGIVE THE MEN WHO WOUNDED THEM SO DEEPLY.

THE HEALING DOES NOT COME ALL AT ONCE. THE PAIN, ANGER, GUILT ... THESE THINGS TAKE TIME.

BUT, AS ALWAYS, ADEL AND METHU CONTINUE TO HAVE HOPE.

THE END

RESTRICTED NATION

This includes countries where government policy or practice prevents Christians from obtaining Bibles or other Christian literature. Also included are countries with government-sanctioned circumstances or anti-Christian laws that lead to Christians being harassed, imprisoned, killed or deprived of possessions or liberties because of their witness.

HOSTILE AREA

This includes large areas in nations where governments consistently attempt to provide protection for the Christian population, but Christians are victims of violence because of their witness.

Who will you pray for today?

Christian persecution is real, and it's going on today. Here's what you can do:

1. **Pray** for Christians suffering persecution around the world. Pray they will be encouraged, and will remain faithful in spite of their suffering. Pray for their persecutors to see the truth of the gospel and to come to know Christ.

2. **Learn more.** Sign up to get VOM's free monthly newsletter at www.persecution.com, or by calling 1-800-75-VOICE. Tell your pastor, your Sunday School class and your friends what's going on with our persecuted family, and encourage them to join you in prayer.

3. **Get involved.** Write letters to Christians in prison. Pack relief goods into an Action Pack for Christian families persecuted in Muslim nations. Mail New Testaments to China or other nations. Learn more about the ways you can directly help persecuted Christians at www.persecution.com.

"What God has joined together, let no man tear asunder."
THE RECEPTION IS FAR FROM WARM ...
IT IS A HOPELESS BATTLE.
Faith that withstood even the fiercest persecution
Hope that a dramatic rescue could be made
Love that refused to give up!
WHERE ARE THE CHRISTIANS HIDING?
I RECOGNIZE YOU. YOU CAME TO OUR VILLAGE, PREACHING PEACE!
ANSWER ME!
ADEL KNOWS THE ANSWER. AND SHE ALSO KNOWS THAT IF SHE GIVES THIS MAN THE ANSWER, WIL BE GIVING HIM METHU AS WELL.
I WILL DIE FIRST.
YOU WILL TELL US WHERE THEY ARE!
SPIT IT OUT, AND I WILL FORCE IT IN AGAIN!
The Voice of the Martyrs
ISBN 978-0-88264-051-8
90000 >
9 780882 640518